Lookin' in All the Wrong Places

THE DR. CAGE CHRONICLES:
MEMOIRS OF A SEX THERAPIST

Lookin' in All the Wrong Places

GRAYSON ACE

4 Horsemen
Publications, Inc.

Dedicated to Drew, Dina, Hope & Katlyn.

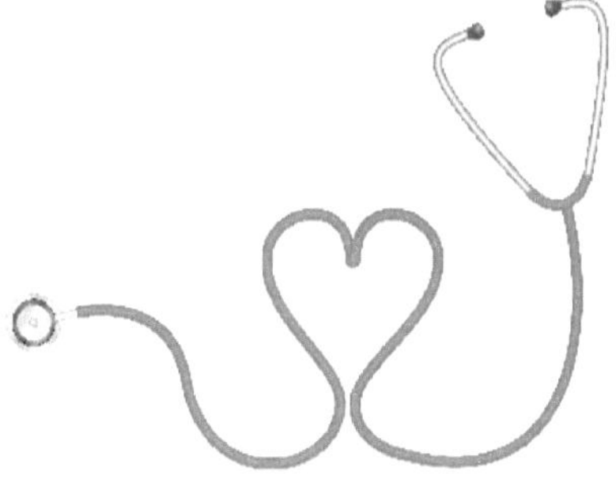

FOREWORD

For those following The Dr. Cage Chronicles, this book includes a new character not featured in previous books. However, Dr. Cage's acquaintance debuts in "Nick" (Grayson Ace's short story in *Unwrap Me: An XXX-mas Collection*), and if you want the juicy details about him, consider adding it to your To-Be-Read list.

"Okay, was this some sort of joke? Sexy St. Nick's name was actually Nick?"

Chapter 1

TRUE LOVE?

Despite meeting Drew's awful friends, I felt like I had hit the jackpot with him. He was charming, handsome, had a hilarious sense of humor, and lit up any room he entered. And the sex, well, the sex was amazing. For the first few months of our relationship, we were living in different cities, so every weekend was like a little game—a chance to have more sex than the prior weekend.

The sex was phenomenal. Sometimes we would role play. Sometimes we would just blow each other. Even though he was pretty much a complete bottom, I figured I'd be able to change that, or at least try to. After all, I've been able to change others.

During my relationship with Drew, I decided not to hold my standard sessions with my patients, and by "standard sessions," I mean I decided that I would no longer fuck any of them. This was real love, and I wanted to make sure nothing I did would stand in the way.

After a few months of dating each other, I knew it was time to take our relationship to the next level and ask him to move in with me. I didn't even finish asking the questions when he blurted out "Yes!" and jumped into my arms. He literally drove home and began packing, and within two weeks, he had transferred his job, and we were playing househusbands. Luckily, Jackie was pretty fond of him, so she didn't mind that he moved in with us.

The day he moved in, he told me he had something special planned for that night, and I figured it was probably related to sex. After unpacking his stuff all day long, I jumped in the shower because I was pretty rank. When I got out of the shower, the room was dimly lit by a bunch of candles all over the place. I wrapped my towel around my waist and walked into the bedroom to see Drew sitting in the corner chair holding two glasses of champagne.

He handed me a glass, and we toasted before taking a sip. Drew was still sitting down, so I placed my glass on the table and straddled my legs over him in the chair, wrapping my arms around his neck. He grabbed the back of my head, pulled me in, and started gently kissing my lips. Drew excelled at romantic kisses.

We kissed for several minutes, wrestling our tongues around one another. My towel was starting to slip off, and I could feel his cock growing in his pants. I started thrusting my hips ever so lightly so I could feel his dick against mine. I didn't take any time before my dick was popping up through the opening in my towel. He grabbed my hips to raise me up off of him, stood up, and walked me over to the bed.

I lay down on the bed, and he pulled my towel off. He took off his clothes, exposing his raging boner, then got on top of me and started kissing again, this time moving from my lips to my neck and down my chest. He kissed around my belly button while playing with my nipples, and slowly made his way down to the tip of my dick. He kept kissing my stomach, purposely making his chin hair rub against my head, which was super ticklish.

Drew stuck out his tongue on the tip of my cock and just barely licked it, then out of nowhere put the entire thing in his mouth. He jerked on his own dick as he moved his head up and down on mine, grabbing my balls and licking them while stroking my dick. I grabbed the back of his head and started thrusting my dick into his throat, listening to him gag as he came back up for air.

He sucked on my tool for a few more minutes then came up and straddled my chest, putting his dick right in my mouth. I leaned forward and opened wide, gladly receiving his beautiful cock. I grabbed onto the base and started stroking it as I sucked up and down. He grabbed onto the back of my head and tilted his body forward so he could face fuck me, which really got me going. I could feel my dick get rock hard, and I grabbed onto it and started stroking. I was so ready to fuck his hole and didn't want to wait any longer.

I pushed him back to get his dick out of my mouth and said, "It's time to fuck." He leaned over to the nightstand to grab the lube, and I held my hand out so he could give it to me. He looked at me and smiled but shook his head no. I was a little confused, but I was open to see his plan. To my absolute surprise, he started pouring the lube on his own dick, then put some on his fingers and shoved them into my hole.

Was this happening? Was this bottom about to top?

"I told you I had something special planned."

He lay down next to me and told me to get on top. I was more than eager and willing to take his massive cock in my hole. I got on top of him and positioned myself so I could feel his dick on my hole. Once they connected, I slowly started lowering myself down when Drew let out a loud gasp.

"What's wrong? Did I hurt you?"

His loud gasp quickly came to an end, and he had a look of disappointment on his face.

"Umm, I just came."

You've got to be fucking kidding me. I didn't even get a whole pump in my hole.

I sat there for a minute, not wanting to make him feel bad and just told him that it was okay. I lifted myself off his dick, and sure enough, he came, and there was jizz leaking from my hole.

I lay down on the bed next to him, leaned over, and started kissing him. I was still rock hard and needed to get off—badly. I grabbed his head and shoved it down into my lap, holding the back of his head and his chin while I forced my dick in and out of his mouth. It didn't take much, and before I knew it, I was shooting my load down his throat. He swallowed every last drop, then started laughing.

"I don't think I'll be topping again anytime soon."

And that was the first and last time Drew every tried topping—at least with me.

Chapter 2

THE FRIENDS

I'll never forget the highest number of times we had sex in one day: seven. I never imagined I'd meet someone who I was this compatible with and this sexually attracted to. Part of my reasoning for leaving PA and moving to San Fran was to find true love—and I finally did. I had the most amazing man, our sex was fire, and we were living the happiest little life.

Drew was the life of the party. He had so many friends, and I was lucky he wanted to bring me into his friend groups. He had his school friends and his work friends, and they seemed to mix pretty well, in spite of them being so different.

One thing I did notice about Drew's friends is that they were all pretty much, well, ugly. And a bit overweight. I never brought this up to him, but I felt like Drew had some type of complex and liked surrounding himself with ugly people to make himself feel better. Or maybe he felt like he was doing some charity work by letting these bitches be seen in public with him, essentially boosting their egos a little bit. "Like, oh my god—I'm with Drew" type of behavior.

The weekend after he moved in, he asked if I wanted to go out with some of his friends. He said that I was super important to him, and that he wanted me to feel like his friends were my friends, and naturally, I wanted the same thing. We made plans for them to come into town and meet at a local bar. I told him that they were welcome to stay at my place, but luckily, they ended up booking their own hotel.

We walked into the bar, and as soon as I saw them, I knew that this was going to be an interesting night. They literally had the same looks on their faces that they had the first time I had met them. Way to make me feel welcome. It was like walking into a den of lions. But instead of lions, they were just cunts.

As I walked toward the table, I couldn't help but judge each of them.

Hope looked like she had permanent RBF: Resting Bitch Face. She was twirling her straggly looking hair and chewing on what I assume was bubble gum. She was a big girl with a huge set of tits. I knew I'd have to make some sly comment to her about them.

Dina appeared to be the prettiest of the three, although that doesn't say much. She had red hair and was fairly skinny, although there was something weird about her legs that I couldn't quite pinpoint. She started to smile when she saw me, but I could immediately tell she was forcing the smile through.

Katlyn was a big girl. As I was walking toward the table, I could hear her voice louder than anyone else in the restaurant. I could tell she was the type of girl who vied for attention.

This was going to be fun.

As I got near the table, they all went from cunts to smiles and got up to give Drew a hug. Dina was the only one who gave me a hug; the other two just kind of smiled and waved. We sat down, and they continued talking to Drew, almost as if I weren't even there. I grabbed the menu and started looking at it, wondering what the strongest drink was that I could order.

As the night went on, they made small talk with me, but it was more of them talking to Drew and asking all about his new life, and barely getting to know me. Drew asked them about their recent trip, and Katlyn basically grabbed a microphone and started reciting what almost seemed like a story.

In her loudest voice: "New Orleans was an absolute shit show. I'm so sorry we couldn't invite you, but it was a girl's trip. I basically got fucked by a stripper."

Drew started laughing, and I damn near spit out my drink.

"Aren't you married?" I asked.

All three of them looked at me as if I had said something totally provocative.

"Yes, I'm married, but it was totally innocent," she continued her story.

"So, Dina insisted that we go to this strip club, and I was already like 17 vodka sodas in, so I was down. We got there, and I saw this super-hot guy in a little yellow banana hammock. I grabbed him and pulled him on top of me and said I only wanted a lap dance from him. He started giving me a lap dance, Hope sat down next to me, and I started rubbing her tits."

Now, we were in a restaurant surrounded my families and little children. I was pretty embarrassed, but everyone else was looking around like nothing was wrong.

"He kept grinding on my junk, and I asked if there was a champagne room we could go to. He grabbed me by the hand and led me to a private room. I turned around and waved for Dina and Hope to come with. The stripper pushed me back down onto the couch, straddled me, and then started smacking my pussy. I had a skirt on and no underwear, and he lifted the skirt so he could smack it more, and he was hitting my clit. I looked over and Dina and Hope were in the corner making out, and at one point Dina started sucking on Hope's tits."

I looked over at Dina and Hope and said, "Drew never told me that you guys were lesbians."

"We're not." They said it in unison. Kind of creepy.

"Let me continue. So, the guy was literally smacking my clit. HE WAS SMACKING MY CLIT, and before I knew it, I was squirting all over the place, and he started rubbing it so it would squirt even farther. He leaned over and gave me a kiss, and I handed him my credit card and never saw him again. I was like a hit it and quit it type of situation, and my skirt was soaking went from all the pussy juice."

She was literally still screaming as she was telling the story. I noticed a waitress leaning over and talking to a woman at the table next to us, and all I heard was "Her mouth! It's horrible." The woman had a disgusted look on her face, and the waitress turned and looked right at Katlyn.

Before I knew it, the waitress was approaching our table, and I knew this wasn't going to be good.

"Excuse me, but this is a family establishment, and we can't have you talking like this. I'm going to have to ask you to leave."

"But I was just telling my friends a story!" Katlyn shrieked.

"I'm sorry ma'am, but you're going to have to go."

And just like that, I had been kicked out of a restaurant for the first time in my life. Super classy. I didn't say anything as we got up from the table, and I apologized to the woman who had made the complaint. As we walked out, I head the three cunts whispering among themselves, and I swear I heard one of them say "Anthony." I didn't think much of it, said goodbye, and left.

Chapter 3

HOPE

Naturally, I let quite a bit of time pass before I had any interactions with this friend group. I was so embarrassed by Katlyn's behavior. The restaurant we had gotten kicked out of was one of my favorites, and I surely wouldn't show my face around there any time soon. We didn't see much of them as a group, but Hope seemed to come around quite a bit.

It was Christmas Eve, and Hope has messaged Drew asking what we were doing. He told her we were just having a couple friends over and invited her to join us. We knew she didn't want to spend Christmas with her family, and I figured maybe her behavior would be different without the other two in tow.

We had our friends Alex and Scott over. We had met them a few months earlier through a mutual friend, and they actually lived right down the street. They were a super cute couple, and we spent a lot of time with them. It was nice to meet another gay couple who wasn't looking for hookups.

Hope got there a few hours later. She had to work on Christmas Eve, which was probably also part of the reason she didn't want to spend it with her family. She said they were mad that she forgot to request the day off. I asked her where the other two cunts were—obviously I left that word out when I asked the question. She said they were spending the night with their husbands. Not sure how either of them landed husbands, but okay.

We spent the night eating and drinking, and I drank A LOT in order to put up with

Hope and her face. I had gotten chambongs, and between the five of us, we must have polished off 15 bottles of champagne with those things. They were the coolest things—champagne glasses with a curved stem so you could chug. Once we ran out of champagne, we started filling them with moonshine, and that's when I knew I was getting really fucked up.

Scott and Alex left around 1am, and I told Hope she could spend the night since she obviously couldn't drive. I wasn't sure what was happening, but I think she was actually being a little flirty and almost coming on to me. I told her she could sleep on the couch or in the spare room, and Drew and I went to bed.

It was our first Christmas, and I was horny after all the drinking and wanted to fuck. Drew and I got into bed, and I immediately pulled his shorts off and started sucking on his dick. He loved getting his dick sucked, and I loved devouring that thing. I was sucking on it for two or three minutes when I heard the door burst open, and Hope came running into the room. Drew quickly pulled the sheets up over his cock, but I was too drunk to care and didn't bother hiding my goodies.

Hope jumped on the bed, kind of like a little schoolgirl, and said, "Whatcha doing?"

What did she think I was doing? She obviously saw that I had a dick in my mouth when she interrupted.

"Can I join in?"

Drew and I looked at one another. Never in my life did I think of having a threesome with a guy and a girl.

Sure. Why not?

Hope lay on the foot of the bed, and I pulled the sheets down and kept sucking on Drew's dick. She pulled her shirt down to expose her tits, and I'm not going to lie, I kind of wanted to suck on them. I kept sucking on

Drew's dick while she was rubbing her tits, and at one point, she grabbed my cock and started stroking it.

I looked up at her and told her to suck it. She crawled up toward me, wrapped her lips around me, and started sucking. So there we were. My man's dick in my mouth and mine in his best friend's mouth. I wasn't really sure where this was leading. Was she going to watch me fuck Drew? Was I going to fuck her while she sucked on Drew's dick? I really didn't care what we did—I just wanted to get off.

Out of nowhere, Drew started screaming.

"Get out! Get out! Get out of here!"

Hope jumped off the bed and ran down the hallway. I heard the front door slam and knew that she was going to drive home. I didn't even care. I looked at Drew, and he had tears in his eyes.

"I can't believe we just did that. I can't believe my mother isn't talking to me."

He started crying like a baby, and I knew he was having some sort of meltdown. His mother stopped talking to him because he chose his dad's side in their divorce, and she was also against him being gay. I held him in my arms while he balled, and eventually we just fell asleep.

Merry Christmas to me.

Chapter 4

THE END

*A*fter the Christmas Eve fiasco, things definitely seemed weird between Drew and me. He seemed rather distant and started spending a lot of time at the gym after work. He had always enjoyed working out, but he normally would ask me to go, and then he just stopped. I knew it had something to do with what had happened with Hope, but I certainly didn't think something like that would get in the way of our relationship.

But then our sex life quickly changed. We went from having sex at least five times a week to not even five times a month. Regardless of what had happened with Hope, this wasn't normal, and I really had no clue what was going on.

One night, while having dinner, Drew seemed to be glued to his phone. We never had our phones at the dinner table, and I started to suspect that something was going on. He got up to grab something from the kitchen, and when I saw his phone go off, I leaned over to see who it was.

Anthony.

Suddenly, it hit me. I remembered hearing the three cunts whisper Anthony's name the night that we had gotten kicked out of the restaurant. Drew had told me about Anthony before, swearing that they were just friends and nothing had ever happened between them. I always found this hard to believe because Drew literally had no gay friends, and I was surprised to see them texting because he said they didn't talk anymore.

I decided to follow Drew to the gym one day. I couldn't believe that things had come to that. I couldn't believe that I was in a relationship with someone I didn't trust and was sneaking around to see what I would find. I waited outside in the parking lot for nearly two hours for Drew to finish his workout.

And then he walked out.

With Anthony.

The moment I saw him walking with Anthony, I was ready to put my car in drive and haul ass out of there. But I waited. I wanted to see how they interacted with one another. Drew walked up to his car, opened the door, and stood there while they talked. What the fuck could they be talking about? They had just spent two hours working out together! I noticed Anthony kept itching his dick and knew that they must have done something in the locker room.

And then it happened. Drew gave Anthony a kiss goodbye.

My mouth dropped. I started bawling my eyes out. It was over. Everything we had was over. I had wasted nearly a year with this guy, and he couldn't even be honest about things. I sped home as fast as I could and just sat in the living room waiting for him. He walked in and acted as if nothing had happened.

"I saw you kiss Anthony."

He didn't even have the balls to look me in the eyes.

"I'll pack my things."

Within two hours, his things were packed, and he was gone. The love of my life had really ended in disaster, and with just a few words, things were over.

At least one good thing came out of this relationship ending—I was able to get back to my normal therapy sessions and finally get a hard cock shoved up my ass.

Chapter 5

RONNIE

I had put off a lot of my old patients that I had slept with, and while I was with Drew, I only saw new patients. I had a long list of appointment requests and decided I needed to get caught up and get my regulars coming back. The first one on my list was Ronnie, and this time he requested to come into the office.

After I called Ronnie to get his appointment booked, he started making small talk. I asked if he was able to come in that afternoon since I had a cancellation. I didn't really have a cancellation—I just wanted to see him and knew I could get him to fuck me.

"I'm on my way," and then I heard the phone call drop. I knew he was excited.

I went back into my office and shut the door behind me to get some paperwork done. I heard the bells ring on the front door and knew it must be him. I walked over to open up the door to my office and saw Ronnie walking toward me with a huge smile. I could barely even get the word "hello" out of my mouth when Ronnie pushed me back into my office and locked the door behind him.

He didn't say anything—just walked up to me, grabbed my face, and shoved his tongue down my throat. After what I had gone through, I wasn't going to even ask any questions. I wrapped my arms around him and kissed him back, rubbing my hands up and down his back and then frantically unbuttoning his shirt. We stopped kissing and hastily started taking our clothes off. We both wanted it equally as bad.

As soon as Ronnie's underwear dropped, I pushed him onto the couch and flew down in front of him in between his legs. He was still soft, and I took his entire piece in my mouth and started sucking it, dying to feel it grown inside my mouth. It didn't take much bobbing up and down, and within 30 seconds, his dick was attacking the back of my throat.

We were like animals who hadn't eaten in a month. He was thrusting his hips up and down, and I had two fingers shoved up his ass while he slammed that dick into the back of my throat. He pushed me backward onto the floor and jumped up off the couch and down in front of me, taking every inch of my cock in his little mouth. I grabbed onto his hair, forcing his face deeper and deeper. I grabbed his side and spun him around, never letting my dick out of his mouth. I wanted his ass in my face, and I dove my tongue as deep as I could into his hole.

I let my tongue go in and out of his ass, licking all around, biting his cheeks, and fucking it like my tongue was a cock. I really wanted to bottom, but this sexy man made me want to top—his hole was so perfect.

Pushing him off of me, I was about to get up when he pressed me back down onto the floor. He grabbed the lube and started stroking up his cock.

"It's my turn."

He had a huge grin on his face and kept stroking the lube on his dick while he dove in face first to my hole. He used his shoulders to lift my legs and lick my hole until it was nice and wet. He came back up and started kissing me, my legs in the air and him holding onto his cock while he pressed it against my hole.

I wanted him so badly.

Slowly entering me, he gave me a minute for my hole to adjust to his tool. He started thrusting slowly, but I wanted it hard and rough. I told him to fuck me like a man.

He grabbed my legs and held them straight into the air and started going on my ass like a jack hammer. He was fucking me so good, and I couldn't help but scream in ecstasy. I pushed my legs down so I could grab onto my cock and start stroking it. He'd start slowing down a little bit, and I'd grab onto his hips and pull him into me harder and harder. Then he'd pump super-fast again like a boy losing his virginity.

I kept stroking my dick and told him I was getting close. He told me to hold off and let him cum first, so I let go of my dick, and within seconds, I felt him flooding my hole. He let out a few loud moans and thrust his dick in as hard as he could, emptying every last drop. He pulled his cock out of my ass, leaned down, and started sucking on mine.

He shoved two fingers into my hole as was blowing me, and I knew what he wanted. Just as I was about to blow, I grabbed the back of his head and shoved my dick all the way into his throat. He started to gag, but I didn't let up—I wanted my cum shooting straight down his throat, and he took it like a champ.

I walked him to the front of the office, and he said he wanted to make another appointment to talk about something that happened to him a few weeks prior. He pulled out his card to pay for the session, but I refused, telling him this one was on me. He gave me a kiss on the cheek and ran off.

For a moment, I had totally forgotten about Drew and Anthony. But then I got angry and knew exactly what I needed to do.

Chapter 6

SEAN

About a month had passed after my break up with Drew, and I focused on work as much as I could. Truth be told, I was really sad and just wanted to do anything I could to keep my mind off things. Jackie was a really good help, and one Friday night, she finally convinced me that I needed to get out of the house. She took me to one of my favorite bars: Hard Richards.

As soon as we walked in, I saw Nick dancing on the stage. He and I had a whirlwind romance, but he ended up being a "male escort" as they say. I think "whore" describes him much better.

I knew he saw me as soon as I walked in, but I completely ignored that part of the bar and walked over to the other side to get my drink.

We spent a couple hours there, slamming back vodkas, and I somehow ended up collecting about eight phone numbers. I don't know what it was, but guys were literally just walking up to me and handing me pieces of paper with their digits. It's almost as if they knew exactly what I needed. I was feeling kind of horny but didn't want to leave Jackie for a hook-up, so I slammed back my last drink, and we left. I could see Nick jump off the stage out of the corner of my eye, but I really wasn't in the mood for his bullshit, so I hauled ass out of there and into the Uber.

When we got back, Jackie had to pee really bad and sprinted inside without me. I sat outside on the bench for a little bit, just enjoying the cooler weather. I wasn't tired, but at that point, I also didn't feel like going anywhere. I pulled the mound of phone numbers out of my pocket and tossed them in the garbage. I got off the bench and started walking toward the door when I saw a blue BMW come around the corner and stop in front of me.

It was Sean.

What the fuck was this guy doing? I already told him that I wasn't interested. This dude fucked me bareback and then told me he had herpes—after he came in my ass. I really wasn't in the mood, but also thought to myself: That's what condoms are for. He rolled down his window and said that he missed me and couldn't stop thinking about me. It was a little weird. After all, we had only hooked up once. But whatever, I was game. I got into his car and told him to take me to his house.

Sean started making small talk, but I told him I wasn't in the mood to talk and that I was still pissed off about the herpes. "I'm just coming over to fuck and then you're bringing me back home." I figured let's just lay this on the table. I reached over and started rubbing his dick over his pants. I didn't want to waste any time and wanted to make sure he was ready to go as soon as we pulled up to his place.

He leaned his head back a little bit, and even though I really didn't like this guy, I knew what he was packing. Once I could feel his dick getting hard, I unzipped his pants and pulled it out. I began stroking him, nice and slowly, unbuckled my seat belt, leaned over, and put his piece down my throat. I started gagging a little bit but just held it there for a second, feeling it stretch my throat a little bit.

I came up for air, and he grabbed me by my hair and shoved my mouth back down on his cock. I slobbered that eight inches up and down, going down and licking the balls before tonguing my way back up to the tip of his head. Thankfully I didn't feel any bumps; otherwise, I literally would have rolled out of the moving car. I kept on sucking until I felt the car come to a stop, and I knew that we were at his house.

He pulled his car into the garage and shut the door behind us. I pushed him against the door of the car and started making out with him. His pants were still unzipped and his hard cock hung out of them, and I grabbed on and stroked it while I was kissing him. He started unzipping my pants, pulled my dick out, and dropped to his knees to devour that thing. I had to grab onto the roof of the car because his warm mouth on my growing dick felt unbelievable.

I trembled a few times. I wasn't sure what it was about his cocksucking ability, but he was quite impressive. I pulled him up after a few minutes and told him to turn around. I spun him around and pushed him into the side of the car. I bent down, grabbed my wallet out of my pocket, and pulled out a condom. I fucking hated using condoms, but I certainly wasn't going to risk it again.

Our pants were still down around our ankles, and we didn't even bother taking our shirts off. I pulled the condom on over my cock and spit in my hand to use as lube. I'm sure he had lube in his house, and it would have been much easier to get inside of him, but I also enjoyed fucking with just some spit every once in a while. I rubbed my spit-filled hand all over my dick, and then spit again to rub it in his hole. As soon as my fingers went inside his hole, he let out a loud moan.

I pushed him forward again, this time with his arms stretched out over the roof of his car. I kicked his foot to make his legs spread a little bit more, and then I had no mercy—I shoved my cock right into his hole. He let out a scream, and I knew I had hurt him a little bit without using lube. I didn't even care. This was payback for the whole herpes scare. I grabbed onto his hips and shoved my cock in and out of his hole as hard and as fast as I could.

Sean would occasionally reach back and push on my chest, almost as if to try and slow me down, but I acted like I didn't know what he was doing. At one point, I grabbed his arm and held it behind his back, which actually even got my dick harder than it already was. I fucked him against the side of his car for a good five or six minutes, then pulled my dick out, grabbed a blanket off the shelf, and threw it down on the ground.

"Lay down on your back."

Sean got down and laid on his back, and I got down in front of him, grabbing his legs and throwing them over my shoulders, his ass perched slightly in the air against my thighs. I threw his legs way back so I could spit on his hole, then lowered them enough so that I could get my cock back inside. He somehow felt tighter, and I started pumping my dick in and out. This time, he wasn't in any pain and was loving every inch I was giving him.

He was stroking his cock while I continue to fuck him, and he didn't even give me any warning that he was getting close. He somehow pointed his hard dick toward me and shot his load all over my shirt. I didn't even care, and honestly, he knew I was a bit of a cum whore.

I fucked him for another minute, and when I knew I was getting close, I pulled my dick out and tore off the condom. I stood up over him and started stroking my cock, and he sat up with his mouth open, not too far from where I was jerking. My intention was to just cum all over him, but if he wanted it on his face, I was going to give it to him. I got super close to his mouth and busted my load like a hose, the first few shots going in his mouth, and then I backed up a bit so I could cover his face.

He grabbed my dick and sucked what was left out of it, and I pushed the cum that was on his cheeks into his mouth. He stood up and tried to kiss me, but I avoided it, bending down to pull up my pants as if I didn't know what he was trying to do. He asked if I wanted a ride home, but I told him I was just going to Uber.

While I was on the way home, I pulled my phone out and saw that I had a message from Nick. What the fuck did he want? I guess I never really made it clear that I never wanted to talk to him again, but he should have just assumed that. I didn't even bother reading the message. I had no time for that fool.

The Uber pulled up to my place, and when I got out of the car, I noticed a guy standing by the door in red shorts and a red T-shirt. It was fucking Nick, and although I wasn't very happy to see him, I couldn't help but be captivated by his muscles—he was pretty much bursting out of his shirt. He looked at me and smiled, and I really didn't know what to say. This man was gorgeous, but honestly, I hated him for what he did to me.

"Follow me."

I walked around the side of the building toward the service entrance. It was a secluded area, and I knew no one would interrupt. I pushed him against the door, dropped down to my knees in front of him, and pulled his shorts down, exposing that beautiful cock. He grabbed onto me as if he didn't want it, but I smacked his hand and told him to relax.

Taking his entire soft cock in my mouth, I started massaging it with my tongue, pulling my lips against it and then opening my mouth to take the entire thing again. I noticed him tip his head back and knew he wasn't going to try to stop me again. I would have rather invited him in for a good dicking, but I knew my dick smelled like a condom, and I didn't want him to think I was a slut.

I stroked on his cock while I was sucking on it, enjoying every single inch he had to give me. He grabbed the back of my head and forced that thing down my throat, and within just a few minutes, I could feel his batter shoot against the back of my throat. He must have been saving it for several days because I couldn't even swallow all of it. Once I let his cock fall out of my mouth, so did half of the little babies that should have slid down my throat.

After wiping my face on his shorts, I got up and ran into the building. He texted me as soon as I got inside asking what my deal was, and I just blocked him. He had fucked me over before, but at least I had gotten all I wanted out of him. Well, at least half of it.

Chapter 7

AN OLD FRIEND

After the night I had just had, I couldn't wait to just get in bed and sleep for at least 12 hours. I'm not sure what was happening, but it seems like after Drew, I couldn't handle dick like I could when I was younger. I was tired, sore, and thirsty. I went into the kitchen to get a bottle of water, then crawled upstairs to my bedroom.

As I was walking down the hallway toward my bedroom, I could hear some noise coming out of Rocky's room. He was still a little slut, bringing a different guy back practically every single night, and it normally didn't bother me. I head another guy's voice, and it sounded vaguely familiar. I normally ignored when Rocky had guys over, but I needed to figure out who this guy was.

Closer to Rocky's room, I could see that the door wasn't entirely closed, which was unusual, because he normally locked it when he had guys over. I set my water bottle down on the ground and tiptoed toward his door. I certainly didn't want him to know I was spying on him. At this point, I could hear some moaning coming from the room, but I couldn't tell if it was Rocky or the other guy.

I leaned against the wall and turned toward his room to peek through the crack in the open door. I saw a muscular guy's back, sitting on Rocky's bed with his back against the foot railing. I could see him holding onto Rocky's head—he was obviously blowing this dude. I saw the guy's arm going up and down, forcing Rocky's head down on his dick. I sat there, watching, and somewhat intrigued by what was going on. Who was this guy? I didn't recognize his back or the back of his head, but I needed to know why his voice sounded familiar.

As I was watching my brother suck this guy's dick, I could feel my own starting to get hard. I wasn't at all in the mood to jerk off, but if what was happening to my brother was turning me on, then why not? I unzipped my pants, pulled my cock out, and started stroking it as I watched my brother blow some hunk. Rocky got up from swallowing this guy's dick and lay down on his back on the other end of the bed. The guy scooted himself up toward him and got down on his chest, ass perched in the air like he was waiting for something. He crawled in between Rocky's legs and started swallowing his dick.

He may be my brother, but he sure had a sexy body and a nice cock. I never thought of Rocky in a sexual way and never fantasized about him, even though we had that threesome once. I had learned in one of my classes that there was nothing wrong with thinking a family member is "sexy." After all, I only thought that he was sexy; the thought of actually having sex with him had never crossed my mind, and it never would.

I kept watching in astonishment and found myself getting super turned on by what I saw. I was slowly stroking my cock because I knew if I went any faster that I'd be blowing my load all over the wall. After a few minutes, Rocky noticed me in the doorway, and I quickly turned so he couldn't see that I was jerking off. I thought he would have called me out, but when I peeked back through the crack, he waved for me to come in, but held up his pointer finger in front of his mouth, signaling me to come in quietly.

I didn't even bother pulling my pants back up. I knew that this was an open invitation to join in. I kicked my pants the rest of the way off in the hallway and slowly opened the door. I quietly made my way over toward the bed, and as I got closer, Rocky shoved the guy's face down, making his cock go deep down his throat. I still couldn't tell who this guy was, and honestly, I didn't care.

The guy thrust his ass in the air, and I'm assuming he knew someone was in the room. I crawled up on the bed behind him, spread his legs, grabbed onto his hips, and dove my face right into his ass. I could barely get my tongue in his hole it was so tight. He started squirming the moment my tongue touched his opening. I licked all around the edges before slowly forcing it deep inside his hole, holding there for a few seconds to let him stretch out.

The stranger kept sucking on Rocky's cock and was forcing his ass back into my face, almost as if he couldn't get enough. After a few minutes of eating his delicious ass, I knew I wanted to get inside of him. It kind of felt like an anonymous hook-up, which I had never done before. I should have flipped him over on his back so I could see who he was, but at this point, I was pretty excited about the anonymity of it.

I pulled my face up out of his ass and made my way up toward him. I ripped my shirt off, and Rocky knew I was ready to fuck him and tossed me the lube. I grabbed the guy's hips and pulled his ass up in the air toward me. I lubed up my dick, rubbed some on his hole, and slowly guided the tip of my dick inside. This dude never once let Rocky's cock fall out of his mouth.

He had the tightest ass I think I had ever felt.

I didn't want to hurt him, and I could tell he didn't want either of us to know he was in pain, so I just left the tip in for a minute and gave him some time to adjust. I then put it in a little more at a time, each time giving him a moment. Once I was balls deep, I just stayed put and waited for him to start the motion.

When he started moving his ass forward and backward, I knew I could take over. I grabbed onto his hips and started thrusting in a slow motion, gradually getting faster and harder. He was still stroking and sucking on Rocky's dick, and I had no clue how Rocky hadn't already blown his load. All I knew was that I wasn't going to last very long with his tight ass, and I wanted to fill him up.

I could see Rocky starting to squirm as I was fucking this dude, and within a few seconds, he said he was going to blow. The guy went deep down on his cock, Rocky let out a loud sigh of relief, and I knew he was drowning this guy. The dude kept on sucking, not wanting to leave a single drop. This was all I needed to see, and I didn't even give any warning. With one final, hard thrust, I was releasing my milk deep inside the dude's ass. I had literally just done an "anon breeding," and I couldn't have been happier.

I kept pushing my cock in and out, wanting to enjoy every moment of this tight hole. I pulled my dick out after I drained every last drop, and when the guy rolled over on his back, I knew exactly who he was.

Rashid. The top who fucked me and wouldn't let me near his hole. And now I just stretched that shit out.

I smiled a little bit after seeing him. It was almost like an accomplishment. I asked him what changed and made him bottom, and he said it was from some things Rocky had taught him that he had learned from me. Apparently, Rocky actually was learning from working with me!

As Rashid lay on the bed, I noticed his cock was still rock hard and realized he hadn't gotten off yet. Rocky had already jumped in the shower, so naturally I was going to do my part since he had just done me a favor. I grabbed the lube and rubbed it all over his dick, hopped on the bed, and straddled his pelvic area, feet planted in the bed, lowering my hole over his perfectly hard dick.

As soon as his head entered, it brought back memories of the first time we had fucked, and it certainly wasn't disappointing. I didn't even bother getting on my knees to get more comfortable—I wanted his load inside of me. I planted my hands on his chest for support and started bouncing my ass up and down on his dick, enjoying every inch as it nearly destroyed my hole. His dick was huge, but I was obviously no stranger to a big wiener.

He held onto my ass, helping me bounce up and down, and I could feel his dick starting to clench and knew he was about to blow. I started bouncing faster when I felt him thrust his hips up into the air, shooting that first load deep into my hole. He held me up and started pumping his cock in and out, and I could feel the bands of cum fill me up. When he put his hips back down, I swung my legs around, so I was no longer on my feet and leaned forward to start making out with him. I got up off the bed, and as I was grabbing my clothes off the floor, Rashid got up and jumped into the shower with Rocky, not even bothering the close the shower door.

Before I left the bedroom, I leaned into the bathroom to say goodnight but saw that Rocky was already down on his knees in the shower sucking on Rashid's cum-covered dick. I'm hoping he rinsed it off before sticking it in my brother's mouth, but if not, I'm sure Rocky really didn't mind.

Chapter 8

ANTHONY

The next morning, I woke Rocky up and told him he needed to come into the office with me. Right before going to bed, I had checked my messages. I had a huge amount of new client requests, and I couldn't handle them all on my own. Besides, Rocky had been skipping out on work a lot and needed to get back into his routine.

I thought for sure he would have brought up what had happened the night before, but he didn't mention a word. He tended to be like that though, never wanting to talk about sexual adventures, almost like they were a secret. I barely even got the car into park when we pulled in, and he was already running toward the door. I'm not sure if he was feeling weird about what had happened, but I honestly didn't really care either.

I started going over some of my client notes while Rocky went through all the messages and started scheduling their intake sessions. I was so far behind and couldn't figure out how I had fallen so short. I really needed the entire day just to get caught up on all of my notes, so I was relieved when I looked at the schedule and saw that my only client for the day had cancelled.

About an hour after getting to the office, Rocky came to my room and said a new client had requested an emergency appointment. I really didn't want to take any appointments for the day, especially not a new client who was already saying he had an emergency, but after the weekend I had, maybe meeting a new client wouldn't be so bad. I told Rocky to schedule him for the afternoon.

A few hours later, I heard the bell ring and assumed it was my new 911 client. Rocky walked him back to my room, and I introduced myself, shook his hand, and had him take a seat on the couch. He introduced himself as Tony. He was a little shorter than I was with dark hair, very Italian features, and a little bit of chest hair popping out from his shirt. He was actually really cute, but I needed to get that out of my head. I knew I had seen him before but wasn't sure where.

"So, what brings you in here today, Tony?"

Well, my friend...boyfriend actually. Let me back up. I met this guy several years ago through a mutual friend and almost instantly, we became best friends. We messed around a few times but made a pact that it would never lead to anything, and that we'd never bring it up or tell anyone that it happened. So many gay guys fuck all their friends, ya know? We wanted to be different.

A few years had passed, and we didn't speak. My boyfriend dated a few other guys, and then at one point ended up dating a doctor. Not sure how he ended up with a doctor, but I was really happy for him when I found out. I messaged him a couple times, but he told me that his new boyfriend didn't believe that nothing had happened between us and that we really shouldn't be talking, so I just left it alone.

Wow. Tony's story seemed so similar to mine. I was really starting to feel bad for the guy and for what he went through.

About another year passed, and it was right after Christmas last year that we reconnected. We ran into each other at the gym and...

Now this was sounding all too familiar. I stopped paying attention as he was telling his story and just started drawing circles in my notebook.

Tony was Anthony, the guy Drew had cheated on me with.

At that moment, I wasn't really sure what to do. Should I stop the session and make him leave? Should I make up an excuse? Should I tell him who I was? No. None of those. I wanted to continue and see what he would say.

And then one day, he kissed me outside of the gym, and that night, he showed up at my front door, told me that his boyfriend had dumped him, and he needed a place to stay. I thought that's when we were going to finally be in a relationship and make things work. And things did work, for several months. And the sex, well, the sex was really good, even though we were both bottoms.

"Interesting. You're both bottoms? How does that work for you guys?"

It really doesn't. He tried fucking me once and literally came in three seconds.

I couldn't help it, but I actually laughed out loud. Anthony looked at me like I was crazy, and I apologized and said that I actually laughed sometimes as part of a nervous tic I have. In reality, I was just happy to hear that it wasn't only with me.

I fucked him once, but it only lasted for about 30 seconds and then I lost my boner. So all we were really doing was blowing each other and eating ass, and honestly, it started getting old. Then Drew said he had this brilliant plan, and one night asked me to wear a blindfold. I'm really not into blindfolds, but I figured I was willing to try anything, so I did. We got into bed and he put the blindfold on me, and then he rolled me on my stomach. Then, all of a sudden, I felt him on top of me and something entering my hole, which I assumed was a dildo. It felt really good, and he was pushing it in and out at just the right speed. I wish it would have been his real cock because I would have loved to have felt his load inside of me, but I guess I had to accept that this is what our relationship would be.

While he was fucking me with the dildo, suddenly I felt a cock on my lips. I pulled the blindfold off and saw Drew kneeling in front of me with his dick in my face. If he was in front of me, who was fucking me? I quickly turned around and couldn't believe what I saw.

Hope. With a strap-on. Drew's idea of a surprise was to have his nasty best friend fuck me with a strap-on.

I jumped out of bed and started flipping out, mother fucking both of them. I told Hope to get the fuck out, and I never wanted to see her nasty ass again. I wasn't at all surprised that she even owned a strap-on because I always suspected she was a lesbian.

I laughed again and quickly apologized. "Nervous tic." I had always thought that Hope was a lesbian, but the one time I brought it up to Drew, he got super mad at me. But now it had me wondering why Drew had gotten so angry the night we had Hope in bed with us. I wonder if she had her strap-on and was planning to use it that night?

"So what's going on now with you guys?"

Well, after that night, Drew started going to the gym alone. We always go to the gym together, but he started saying that I was interfering with his workout and that he just needed some alone time.

Wow, I could see that Drew was still the same douche bag he was when I was with him.

I started following Drew to the gym. I knew he must have met someone else, probably some total top who could fuck his brains out. But every time Drew would come out of the gym, he was always alone. So, I figured I needed to see what was going on inside. So I literally went into the locker room and hid in one of the lockers in the row that I knew Drew used.

One day after his workout, I could see Drew through the vents grabbing his towel, so I waited until I heard the shower go on and then snuck over to the area. When I got over there, I could hear two voices coming from the stall, and I was immediately devastated. I knew that he was cheating on me.

I ran back over to the locker but left my phone out on one of the benches with the camera on so I could get a picture of the guy and figure out who it was that he was cheating on me with. I got the picture but never recognized the guy. That night, I confronted Drew with it, and he literally said nothing. He packed up his stuff and left. And that's the last time I ever saw the fucker.

"Can you show me the picture?" Anthony grabbed his phone and scrolled through the photos, and I immediately recognized the guy.

It was Rashid. The guy I had fucked the night before.

I laughed again and again blamed it on my "tic." There's no way I was going to tell Anthony who the guy was. I actually kind of felt bad for the little fucker, even though he was the one who ruined my relationship. I was just wondering how he hadn't figured out who I was.

I told Anthony that he needed to make another appointment to come back the following day to see me. I knew just the treatment plan that he needed.

Author Bio

Grayson Ace has had his fair share of sexcapades, and figured why not write about them? Recently divorced, he is re-discovering himself (and plenty of hot men) and creating many new sexy adventures along the way. If you like what you see, please leave a review, and you never know....you may end up in one of the stories!

GraysonAce.com

Facebook: Grayson Ace

Instagram: graysonaceofficial

Twitter: @GraysonAce1

More Books From
Grayson Ace

How I Got Here

First Year Out of the Closet

You're Only a Top?

You're Only a Bottom?

I Think I'm a Serial Swiper

Lookin' in All the Wrong Places

What Makes Me a Whore?

A Breach in Confidentiality

Back Door Pass

My European Adventure

An Unexpected Affair

More to come!

4 Horsemen Publications LGBT Erotica

Leo Sparx
Before Alexander
Claiming Alexander
Taming Alexander
Saving Alexander

Erotica

Ali Whippe
Office Hours
Tutoring Center
Athletics
Extra Credit
Bound for Release
Fetish Circuit

Dalia Lance
My Home on Whore Island
Slumming It on Slut Street
Training of the Tramp
The Imperfect Perfection
72% Match
It Was Meant To Be... Or Whatever

CHASTITY VELDT
Molly in Milwaukee
Irene in Indianapolis
Lydia in Louisville
Natasha in Nashville
Alyssa in Atlanta

HONEY CUMMINGS
Sleeping with Sasquatch
Cuddling with Chupacabra
Naked with New Jersey Devil
Laying with the Lady in Blue
Wanton Woman in White
Beating it with Bloody Mary
Beau and Professor Bestialora
The Goat's Gruff
Goldie and Her Three Beards
Pied Piper's Pipe
Princess Pea's Bed
Jack's Beanstalk

4HorsemenPublications.com